With
& Garlic
Victory

J.M.I. Kagan

With Garlic & Victory | *J.M.I. Kagan*

Layout and Cover Design April Osmanof
Cover Art "May 2006" by the author © 2006
© 2008 J.M.I. Kagan
ISBN 978-0-6125-2339-1
for information address:
Firevane@excite.com

Contents

The Rhythm of Hot Grease
and World Peace

As it was I sat there and waited until the owner came and shook my hand. We headed to the back of the restaurant and pulled out a couple of chairs. "So" he said, "tell me about the last place you worked."

"It was a good place, the owner was fair," I said."We cooked burgers, steaks, fish & chips... the usual."

"I see—and the others?"

"Well, to be honest, I've worked in the larger places. Three level kitchens, high end food, 15 people in the kitchen."

"So why do you want to work here?" he stretched out on the seat, arms folded, his face betrayed the countenance of a man suffering with hot grease on his balls and a spatula broken off in his ass, but was too uncomfortable with my being there to scratch.

"Well", I said "I'm new in town and times are hard so..."

"Well, as an employer, it's hard to hear I was your last resort. "He stared at me. "Listen I can take one look at you and see you won't fit in here." I grabbed my keys and stood up.

"THAT'S IT?—you called me all the way out here for a two minute interview? hoping I'd tell you my dream in life, my true aspiration, was to flip burgers? What kind of asshole are you?"

I walked out.

I went to the next place, the same grease coated walls, the same poker machines, and relatives of the drunk from the last bar straining their eyes on the torn and stained rug. The guy (owner) comes up to me, looks me up and down. I was desperate, I needed money. So with my lips wired into a smile we headed for the ubiquitous office restaurant, the dark end of the bar. We sat down.

"So." I fished for his name, starting with my hand out.

"Walter, Walter Stimple," he shook my hand.

"Walter, what do you need to hear to finalize this thing?"

"To start, your qualifications"

"I worked in a bar back in Baltimore, it was just like this one" I lied.

"Really? And how did you like it there?"

"Wonderful—one of the best times in my life." Here I wasn't embellishing much; I was paid under the table. Worked some bar shifts, and was pouring or being fed drinks nightly by the bartender, myself, my friends or their rich spouses. I knew I was lucky but I didn't think lightning would strike twice this easily.

"Let me ask you..."

Here it comes, I thought, can he smell the alcohol on my breath?

"Why do you—"

Oh Christ! Big smile.

"—want to work here?"

"I've always romanticized about cooking in a fast food environment while working for world peace," I blurted, "I think I can accomplish both here."

Silence.

"Are you making fun of me?"

"No"

He glanced at me sideways, "okay then," then began a smile, "I'll check your references and then you can come in tomorrow and we'll show you around." He took my papers and walked into the kitchen. Relief filled my head and I needed a beer to celebrate. I was going to segue over to the bar but thought better of it and moved on down the street.

10 Count

Warm.

Quiet.

Bar's half way there.

My first
 beer.

Drawings done

Paintings are working
  and lined up

A girl, 20, at the house

A quiet boss

Belly full

Friends calling

Scotch coming up

Not a bad day

The Telegram

Love has decided it's not enough
to live upstairs and laugh at me
while it strokes young thighs in my direction

Now he's sending
Personal telegrams to the house
—he couldn't make it—
by long-haired girls of no more than 21
to my door, knocking.
"Yes?" I answer, a warm can of beer in my hand.
"You must be Kough"
"And?"
"I've been sent to give you this"
She hands me the envelope
I read the letter
while I pin the cat that's trying to escape out the door
between my legs.
"So Mr. Kough" she purrs, —the delivery girl,
not the cat—
"You understand?"
"Yes I get it"
"Thank you Mr. Kough" she says with her pure white smile
and a careless tilted head.
She closes the screen door.
Love must be a crazy *woman*
Who else would think to torment a man through the
mail.

A Job

The job is like a void, a vacuum
Sucking in everything
It makes a dull sound in the ear
Irresistible it pulls you
To it like a line forming to the right of the gallows
And as I drive I can't help
But think, or imagine,
How lucky Antoinette was
She never saw it coming
Quick and done
No more thoughts
Or nightmares
While my treason against labor eats at me
Sucks rather,
An ice cold drink
through a straw.

Knuckle Dragon

I am the slob
The ugly, bad, and embarrassing.
The Drunk.
I laugh out loud at the mirror
Red faced, hair in all directions
As I urinate, damn! piss everywhere
Most into the bowl
Disgusting
But able to read.
Intolerable, with fits of lucidity.
Pathetic or enviable?
The one who has found all the worth in words
And paints,
But not
In financial security.
but believe me, the strong still whip the weak
like a charging bull between barrels.
like the animal tattoo
That snarls fire
clawing and swirling
up mean men's arms.

Chauvinist Near Dawn

sometimes you drink and drink and drink
and women seem so far away
that you start making plans for something else
start looking to the accomplishments of other men
find your own way among men
women are:
non linear,
self serving,
poor chess players.
machines.
Finesse in life is theirs alone

you read your own writing
find yourself disgusting
spin the platen
ball up the paper and those words
and discard it
you look into the mirror and see yourself
as abnormal and as adjusted as to be expected
open a Natty Boh' at 4 a.m.
pet the cat and listen to rock and roll at full volume
and wonder what could have made you write such a thing.

Fortune

Mid july
resigned to selling poems
door to door
by mail order or
bartering

I think to myself
sometimes a man just needs a beer
a place to sleep and a virgin
or better still a sexual encyclopedia
with two long legs
painted lips and a penchant for whiskey

getting even with all my hopeful teachers
and councilors
I have ended up doing what I wanted
I have cheated the job market out of a living
I sit
do crossword puzzles
read and write poetry
eat a bit,
drink red wine from
the box
kept atop the ovens
and still manage
every Friday
to pick up
a paycheck before leaving my job

luck still exists in this world
so I'll stand here feeling sick
as I watch the wheel of fortune spinning
-or is it me?-

between mailings,
I stagger house to house with the poems. Absently
wondering if lady luck will grant a brunette to
deliver me five bucks

a guy appears in the doorway, head spinning, lost
in his own spirals
he leans over me
    "five bucks is nothin' buddy," he snaps his
    fingers, "Brunettes' a dime a dozen"
his pigeon head chokes twice then confides in my ear
    "if you get the chance to take a snap shot of her passed
    out on your door step with her panties around her
    ankles with five dollars in her hands,
      that, buddy… that's luck"

Leaving a Job ──────────

It's been almost a month and a half since
I had time in the room,
my room,
with paintings and writings scattered
over the floor, and the sheets,
the tables, counters.
Leaving a job where men are ground into
paste,
where other men take pride in being
tough enough to take the heat
and the sweat,
 the condescension.
Hours and hours of misfortune.
Complemented by the daisy staff:
of managers, the waitresses,
even the busboys
who work in air-conditioning a few days a week
making all that money
and getting all that ass.

* * *

Sometimes the bottle just makes more sense
faced with all this work to do
the painting and the writing
I wish I didn't have such a stranglehold on making
things.
Maybe a few days away from my zoo
will help
I make the call
away from men
desperate enough to believe in eating shit
and being held under the knife,
who claim indifference, yet delicately mollify their
words
–Purpose for confused braggarts–
CHRIST!
If I did nothing, I'd rather sit under a tree and
drink beer
or ride my bicycle
than truly
work on going back to a job

Girls

The one they called Chicky,
the stinking cook
knew that women leave
all the time
and that his time is better spent remembering the
taste of himself
The girls turn away
leave for themselves
only for themselves
always for themselves
never charitable
The cook steps back smears his hands on his apron and
swan dives through
the neck
of a bottle
of Jim Beam
His lungs fill
heart pounds
—surviving a bit longer—
brains slowing
his eyes close
on amber.

Dead Dad

* * * * * * * * *

My father died of a heart attack.
He ate and drank and loved his family.
He only hit me once.
after I, riding my *Big Wheel*,
Too engrossed to notice,
ending up under the wheel well of a car
he held me very tight at arms length,
tears in his eyes, and he hit me
so hard we all froze:
me mom and dad.
And even then I knew why he hit me,
because he was still able to.
There was something still left inside me to hit;
I survived

* * * * * * * * *

He lost his work—
there were no more columns to edit,
no more games or sentences to be watched,
cared for, or followed.
I rarely saw him
but I do remember him trying to teach me
how to throw a curve ball,
his giant hand spreading my fingers across the laces.
I remember the paper closed.
There was a big party.
I remember getting things from his office.
Past the huge print rollers
filing cabinets and letter boxes
we buried him
there were food and cards
and neighbors
they closed the paper
he died

* * * * * * * * *

I ride my bike to work
I eat soup
and bread
and drink cold red wine
and I think,
What will be my demise—
the coffee that I drink,
the pills I take,
the heartache?
Lost women
or the lost jobs?
I'm son and heir to a weak heart
and I wonder what it will take to crack mine.

—— Health and Fitness ——

Sometimes I take it line by line.
like that line

sometimes you find yourself having trouble
separating yourself from others
sorting it all out,
sorting YOU out,
Because their answers never work.
where they end is a science
where you begin is art

And when others corrected me, I resisted
because their answers were not safe,
extending their hands toward the slaugter.
everytime they corrected me they were attempting to
finish me off for my own good.

I wish sometimes I could make poems like Bukowski
finding them all over the house, the yard, between
books under beer
finding them, losing them
and finding more.
The man didn't worry; they came as they went. some
real stinkers,
and then there was some beauty.
but he never sought it out, he never tried to control
it
poems, ponies, women, all calculated gambles
I wish I was as lucky

For some there is no solace
Nothing, until you corner it
in an empty quiet room
white, but for the soot.
At first you're on the attack,
then it has you at its mercy on the floor,
you pour beer on your head
like greek wrestlers and their olive oil
to slip from its grasp
I spend time every day medicating myself against
others' sicknesses
healthy in the head, a pruning clarity in the eye

It's when things get stuck, sickness moves in.

health is cleanliness.
I was never particularly clean;
I always had to clean myself.
I was never right; I always had to correct myself.
life is simple,
so I'll ease myself

Untitled IV

The night before
was bursting with friends and alcohol
beautiful women and billiards

During the day he looked for a job
nothing
turned up

The death that usually sat in the
periphery of his vision
was slowly replaced with depression
slowly encroaching on his sight

At least, he thought, I still have death
in the middle of rain choked traffic
out of his fogged windshield that bruised
night colored figure
slowly warmed his heart

That night his buddies took him out
the girl left her phone number
they brought home another 62 beers.
he had won with arrogance
and the fat end of the cue stick
he drank deep into the morning
and hashed out
five poems

Minute Meter Maid

There is something awfully poetic

About being woken up early

on a sunless day

To drive your girlfriend to a train

In her new car

And the opportunity to

Crush a meter maid

Against the hood of that girlfriend's car

Arises.

Good fortune and relief spread through the vehicle;

As the maid lays limp (as you imagine it)

And accusing

As a parking ticket

Between the windshield

and the wiper blades.

The Lion the Witch
and the Sheetrock Cage

There once was a lion
Big-paunched and full of big ideas
He was prone to idiocy
Undeserved adulation, mood swings
And buying only the cheapest beer and coffee

He was with a very attractive, young, strong willed
Tight bodied, heavily clawed,
  witch

They had decided that it was time for them to start
Sharing the rent, getting a studio, saving money
And getting older

The lion was very proud, some said too proud
And that he made light of everyone and everything.
But those people were stupid and no one cared what
they thought anyway...

They both asked around town, and finally decided
On a studio, on the east side of town
Out by the cemetery
Where the poor children played and hollered in the
street
Late into the night
Under halogen bulbs

It was an old factory and they were given a sweet deal
in exchange for some sweat they could have the space
for almost nothing
provided they built the walls for their studio

On the first day
Both came ready to work
The lion heaved his chest and flared his mighty
shoulders
The beautiful witch grabbed a 120# air gun
And told the lion, "Stay out of the way"

The lion tried to help

Lift something… anything
"listen, baby," said the size 2 witch,
"just stay out of the way.
I'll call you when I need you."

Time went by, the space was cleared
the lion was drinking regularly
And starting a new job, he was finally moving out from
his neck of the woods
He was shooting pool
Lionesses loved him
And all the boy animals wanted to
Stick their sticks
In the young witch which he had chosen

The next day of work started
And it was time to start drilling
But as the lion collected screws
The witch, grabbing a screwgun, began raving,
"Listen, move that wood, no, I said left," then in crazed soprano
"What are you doing with the tape?"
"I said a scant 3!"

the lion wagged his tail at the witch
who was too busy drilling 31/2 inch drywall screws
to notice his ire.
He thought to himself I'm the king of the fucking
jungle.
What the fuck is this?
Angered he finished his coffee walked over to the
neighbor's yard and took a deep shit on their lawn
He wiped his ass and pulled up his skins
Thinking to himself 'fuck everyone'

Day three
The lion steered off lionesses, conservatively drank one beer
Was sleeping properly, setting alarm clocks
Showering, combing hair like a feline possessed
He and the witch had stacked drywall and were
Ready to "throw it up"

They both went for the first piece of sheetrock–
"Listen I'll do this", said the lithe witch, " You go find
something to do, I'll call you when I need you."

the lion grabbed a warm brew, sat on a pile of studs
and watched the birds fly overhead.
The lion suddenly grabbed a construction pencil
And started thinking situations in his head
then slowly wrote them on a stack of scrap shims

at the end of the day the witch stretched her arms,
her pert nipples
and tiny waist.
"well I'm done" she said "lets go home."
The lion though, at the thought of going home with the
Witch, turned foreman, turned witch again,
was slowly going mad.
I may be spending the better part of my life with this
witch, he considered
He made a silent benediction against insanity
Made a kissy face to his witch and said, "yes dear,
let's go home."

But late at night the lion snuck back into the studio
And began some work of his own
The only thing the witch hadn't touched yet
The door knob.

The next day the lion woke to the sound of cackling
The witch was there, satisfaction across her face,
lips curled into a cocksure smile.
The lion had been asleep on the other side of the
studio door
He arose with an immense and dangerous stretch

"You see Lion" said the Witch," You did this without me."
She waved at the door. "Now you're locked in"

With a calm and depth, " It is you who are the fool, Love"
Purred the Lion, "I've finally locked you out"

Mammal Poems

Sometimes I see others
and they're so happy to read poems:
An accomplishment.
even the best poem won't stop hunger
or laziness.
a poem can't stall the landlord
or halt the police.
a poem can't find clarity
or forgive an accident.

poems only crush against the skull
they can feed on anxiety
disturb ideas
and offend relations.

they cause insomnia in the strong
and ego in the weak.

poems are
alley urchins that howl and scream.
that most society hates.
they're hungry, and red
and hide, disturbing the sane
deep into the night.

poems drain
and consolidate, they teethe
and pounce, and claw;
they try to survive.
poems are hard to hate.

Bum Ankle

The leg pain is back
This mystery at the bottom of my shin
Sewn, my ankle, together with a tent stake
And an overhand Fragonard stitch.

I can't afford a doctor
So I'm at the behest of wet floors and cobbled streets
I have no idea what the hell is down there
It looks clean, no punctures
No accidents
I ride a bike because I can't run anymore
And the pain's always gone away before

I remember when they sent me to their chiropractor
To let him take a professional look at it
"Don't they do backs?" I'd said at the time.
But I acquiesced, sitting on his stuffed table
While he'd send electric currents through the leg.

Sometimes when he'd leave the room
Me sitting there, electrodes on my foot
I'd turn the dials up to 10. Just to see if I
Could take it.
And maybe speed up the process.

After the shock treatments the doctor would grab my ankle
Then yank it out of the socket and jam it back in.
At first I thought it was working
But gradually I would nod my head
just to get out of there
Then I stopped going.

I remember the receptionist there.
"Your legs are your foundation," she once said
"And the left side is your female side, your mother's side."
I asked her to lunch. We ate, then made out.
The next time I had an appointment
We'd go to lunch again.
She talked.
about her groups, their mantras, her yoga
Her career with dancing, her age (22)
Her ex-boyfriend.

I couldn't bring myself to interrupt
When she came to the part about her paying her half of
the check.

It just hurts to bend
Walking has become a labor
And I wonder how long the pain will last this time
I put ice and salt water on the thing
I sleep with it up
I drink beer with it flexed and bent
Sometimes the pain splinters up the leg
Interrupting my coffee and early day dreams

My dad had a heart condition
And I think to myself maybe it skipped a generation
And I was only lucky enough to break even
Betting on a strong heart over a bum ankle

No Craziness, Please

These crazy cats

They hate all the ones outside

Sometimes spitting at each other

Plying for affection

Sitting there with their leaping joints

Poised

In furious contempt

Hearing them cry and howl out there in the night

Behind iron doors

No craziness please

Tonight I have to write something

It's Easier to Write

It's easier
to write depressing
and pejorative words
in the year 2003
But you know? I'll make it.
I enjoy swimming in beer and whiskey,
Walking down the street listening to engines
And watching women
Or
Biking through hip-high fields
with cattle and other animals near by
but it's not easy to drink
or roam across green earth
people you desire, enjoy much of nothing
from you
and people you don't care to know
or worse yet, detest,
expect so much more.

Ode to Shannon

It's time I wrote something
where am I?
Jesus! There are notes and torn paper everywhere;
no wonder my head is like a greased anus.
—let's go—

To Shannon for whom I have the utmost respect:
Some people
just don't get along.
All the words are out of order.
They, Them. Those people, drink the wrong drink.
shake with the wrong hand
think with a vulgar mind...
and when the world does go your way.
and they all suck,
dancing on your toes,
drinking your wine,
eating your food,
relaxing in your home.
when they all think you're right
a rock, a modern sculpture.
when they are totally comfortable.
you itch, and bore.
look at others.
thinking to yourself
'they think that's folly?'
then you let them all down
with an even bigger disappointment.

Notes from the Job

Like most thieves
I have little
Produce little
Have little money

scraps
are all I have to hold on to

I am bound to kitchens, lashed to them,
and by them
By the kitchens I've been administered
Burnt, Calloused hands
A twisting ankle
Thinning hair
And insomnia,
Slowly being ground down by coarse people.
We don't belong together.
We at least ought to be separated in different viveria

in the same cold water
aquarium

and then there's women
Always worrying about the beer
The freedom of drink, carousing

Better, they believe, to slowly go mad
at the job.
there is dignity, they believe, in that.

I think it archaic to destroy oneself
At a job.
Rather than

slowly slumping over
From friendship and revelry

The machines have won!

+ Giving Blood +

Giving blood, like anything else unusual, can be a euphoric event. Starting out as a prosaic thrill, a Disneyland of the sanguine kind. Money? I thought, for this stuff? I'm spilling it all day at work and the boss gives me nothing. "Patch it up," (like a tire) he says, "And go back to work." In hindsight neither of us, employee nor employer, was taking advantage of the money being lost. As I see it I'm bleed-ing perfectly useful money all over the place. With the soaring cost of medical coverage coupled with a positive advertisement... my God, I think to myself, what this needs is a piss-hardened shill! What better way to convey a corporate image of hard work, quality, and civic minded virtue. When I think of all the nega-tive news coverage I read in the paper, of corporate chow houses pumping out poisonous food and grinding the fresh work force of America into the unskilled hamburger of tomorrow. I see days when plasma centers and workers compensa-tion get together and corporations pronounce: "When accidents happen we have our employees' backs, and our employees want to give back too, Back to the com-munity! (parenthetically) And they're doing so from bottom of their hearts!"

So this is the daydream-woven reality of donating blood. What an easier way of making money, I thought. I could make 60 bucks in three days, two and a half hours of work. "bah, nothing."

But then reality slowly encroached. The thing was, in the far north-west, money seemed terrified of me. Paychecks barely made it alive from one month to the next. The use of money always brought little plays into my head, scenarios of myself clutching pennies while searching for loose change in seat cushions and telephone booths. Food and beer, of course, cut deepest. Using myself as a soft thimble though, I protected an anemic wallet from frequent pricks. Fortunately for some of us, libraries out there were replete and free.

I'd have to drive to ZBT laboratories. A blank shop in the forgotten section of a mall, between a Mexican tortilleria and a cigarette outlet. The whole strip of storefronts was at the bottom of black and towering fir trees. I'd pass two schools, a golf course, two libraries, and three major arteries to get to that place. Walk-ing in was like entering into school detention. or a veterinarian's laboratory. The walls were painted yellow, not bright enough to gladden, and not neutral enough to calm. The color instilled a sensation of humidity: of sweating human bodies packed too tightly.

The place was staffed by jaded nurses and wall mounted TVs to slow down minds along with pulses and nervous systems. I'd wait, then wait some more, as all health professionals seem to prescribe. The younger men sat with slack jaws and trepidation, scheming to entice young pussy. The older and experienced pro-ceeded with book, the crossword, or the paper. Soon you'd be called and directed to individual cubbies where they'd weigh you, paint you —a bit of iridescent nail polish on the pinky- then send you for the tests. Now, true monotony would begin. Picture; the nurse, a girl, young and stiff, believes herself to be educated and useful, a dull, unconcerned low income meat sticker. Completely soulless. Or the older women, spending their entire lives getting to this place, in hopes of dying here, I suppose, old enough to get the joke of this exhibition. The young nurses would look down their white coats as if they're going someplace I wasn't able. The mature nurse, the initiated, simply played along.

A nurse will prick your finger, take your temperature, your blood pressure, scan your blood centrifuge, and read off the list of high risk activities. Now, the speech, at this point takes place like second nature. Questions like; Do you drink? Have you gotten a filthy tattoo recently? Do you jerk off? Any surgery? Mother's maiden name? Where do you live? Do you sleep with whores? Use needles? The women, and they're all women, maybe one fag doctor haunts the halls, they're doing this at machine gun speed while taking blood, measuring, weighing, what have you, while reusing the same canned speech visit after visit. Usually it's the young, sanctimonious, or misguided that read slowly. It's all bullshit. The older nurses understand, everyone in the room is here for the money. Donors simply wait for the pauses so that you can give the ubiquitous "no" at each question. Nurses then ramble on with their questionnaire, every man listening for the one long pause, the pause that suggests that you answer, "yes" to the previously asked question so as to get this thing started and get on with getting your money.

The obviousness of the formality exposes the health industry for what it is, precision racketeering. You sign your name with pen and bloody cotton ball in hand.

Now I get called and hooked up. If I'm lucky, a quality nurse will stick me, she's usually happy, very tight in her white uniform and on the cusp of flirtatiousness. If her boyfriend or the doctors can't make her feel pretty then I can, anything to enhance my desirability. If the odds are against me I may get the south east Asian doctoral left over, or Hilda with the enormous thumbs, or Carl, one of the few males on the staff, who looks like a dying rape victim. Some failed experiment I picture more easily in a lab than in a lab coat. They start by seating me in a scooped green lounge chair, medicinal, and frightening. One of the nurses comes over. Again if I'm lucky she comes straight over. If I'm not, she's probably dealing with a 300 pound fainter or squirter. Or some hysterical woman scratching at her arm trying to remove the needle, all this, of course, cuts into my hourly rate.

First they smear the iodine, a cold brown sauce, slowly applying it in rhythmic circles the swab sliding and rolling off the fist-tightened and exposed vein: A circling of the prey. The anticipation makes some of the strong squirm. Next they tape on the blood pressure cuff. Then comes the needle, plunged in. All the intensity of the nurse, the machine beeping and whirring crazy is for nothing. The puncture's really not so bad. I sit there in tough-guy grace, realizing that somebody's three years of nursing school led to this, this one action, skewering the vein. Growing accustomed now, to the steel twitching in my arm, I sit back and make money. What happens is, the machine kicks in, something like a small vacuum pump to match the one in my chest. The arm band inflates and the machine starts taking my life, slowly working it up the tubing, smearing the inside of the centrifuge, separating life from plasma. Money from life. I'm instructed to pump my fist. I conjure an image of what seems to be the needle working its way through the vein, into the meat. I think to myself, "its only so thick, Jesus! I'm going to accidentally kill myself, or lose an arm. There's simply too many things that could go wrong" all the blood runs cold as the steel touches it, and chills the rest of the circulation. You see the machine working. You begin pumping your hand with misgiving, then the machine exhales and begins pumping the blood back in. Is an aneurysm possible? "No, I hope." Just then the equipment beeps pure insanity. Flashing yellow, green. Nurses start running over, turning off the machine and flicking the buttons frantically, "Mister Kough, you need to flex your fist or this is not going to work" Jesus, I think, they're only interested in this for my plasma, this is no joke! Let the fucking guinea pig out.

The blood, legally bound at this point, heads back to the rightful machine. Then my gums begin to feel as if they're receding to the point where the teeth are in danger of falling out. The machine cracks off and the cuff inflates again, the green lights light up and you're off, pumping wildly for the cherished end of 20 dollars and your life. Forty-five minutes later, lips buzzing, the sodium chloride pumps back into me like iced tea, creating the feeling of condensation on the arteries. At last the money and my life are in sight. As the taste of tin creeps into my mouth, I am finally extricated from the machine. Harnesses are released, needles removed, more signatures, and I am given a little tag with which to claim my money. At this point there's more waiting. Doctor's orders? Of course there's no rush for pay outs, there's now a long line of fresh guinea pigs to prep, so we sit or stand there, holding cotton balls in the crook of our arms, waiting.

After getting our money, most of the men and women hit the cigarette outlet next door. Usually I go to the grocery, to buy beer, bread, maybe some pasta or cheese. Ignorantly, when I arrived out here I thought I'd be buying beer with recycled cans. Not realizing recycling was required, and that you paid for it each time you bought beer. When you recycled, all you did was recoup your deposit.

Back at the house, I'd think, "Well, I'm alive, still," and I took pride in that. A bit of adventure every two or three days was a show of resourcefulness. Now when I had dreams of the immediate future at least I had beer in them. At a bar with some pocket change, I even saw visions of myself at the dog track. Most importantly, I was surviving, and still able to produce the work. I was still moving forward. I thought, "If a man can't do that, He's lost."

Half-Wit Army

I was living again. I had moved out from the old place. I was a man who would look in the mirror daily, but was unable to laugh at himself. Living in a time of joyful conservatives, and the nations' anarchists phlegmatic. Hunter S. Thompson had died.

But again, I was alive, and with a girl. She made out with everything. She was always kissing everything; hands, feet, elbows, ears, frenching my bellybutton, genitals, you name it. She had much free time and enjoyed making things with wood. I would curry favor with her by buying electric saws and routers.

I had run into an old friend from California, Jacob Kough. He was living the high life, playing in Hollywood, nearly a billion in the bank. He confided in me once, " It takes audacity to think yourself worthy of being the president. Me on the other hand, I have an aptitude for success." He'd done it all with the help of his army of halfwits.

It all started as a joke, this half-wit army. He'd get them working at the job, just a dishwasher, nothing special, but he would take time after work, an hour sometimes, just to show them how to peel an onion, slice some bologna. That army of his, his half-wits. They'd get a call and the feeling was like a little rainbow, a nightlight that wouldn't go off, all the points of the compass would converge for them, and a soft sound, high like sneakers on a basketball court or a kettle whistle would be followed by a deep murmur, like getting on an underground train. After years of this private kitchen tutorage and with some money under his belt, he decided to bring on investors.

He had the gift; of inner glow, hyperbole, and of making others feel heroic. Those were the newly initiated back then, the *nouveau riche* of the back alley movers and the slack happy shakers. He coerced them all.

He was bringing on five, six, eight guys. Paying them pennies compared to their 'educated' counterparts. He would teach them, and I mean TEACH them. The man had the patience of the saints. And they loved him. Pinheads, retards, the addled, they all truly loved him, the whole place was nearly run by them at that point. Little jobs each of them, but with half-wit care and consideration. They cut onions, toasted hamburger buns, cleaned with love and devotion. Jake gave them all loving smiles and pats on the back. His partners, the drug addled and the merely dull all made their money back in record time, then all Jake did was ask for more money. They built restaurants, delis, coffee bars, and in each he gave himself, and his quiet heart, in return for carefully ground beans, babied French fries, and painstakingly made bagels with treasured lox. After awhile even the partially limbed were looking for work, the blind, the deaf too.

Investors were like sunshine all beating down rays of credit on Jake. Jake thought of himself as a writer though. He never comfortably wore the entrepreneur pin on his sleeve. Writing was his passion, along with those idiotic melodies and depraved tunes of his.

Now with literally thousands of cafés, delicatessens, and burger chains, Jake decided to turn toward himself. He started bringing some of the half-wits home with him and after more dedicated tutoring, they were doing odd jobs around the house. Most were from the première restaurant and with him for years. One day he had an idea and began giving them new jobs. He had three that were particularly close to him; Toby, Darell and Cheeks, and with his extreme patience they began writing; parts for plays, mini series outlines, biographies, others worked in character development. Soon there were 200 latchkey kids on the property, fifty just to feed the other 150 binkos. One I remember, Jessie, had a simple job. She held a rubber stamp high above her head and, on the reverse, was written, in fancy handwriting, Jakob Kough. And she would bring it down with tremendous unbeknownst strength on the bottom of all of Jake's memos, dramas, plays, etc. And they all were driven like salivating horses, with fondness and pure loving thanks.

Jake was in town visiting his old haunts. He suggested we get some coffee, so he invited me to the top floor of his hotel. It didn't occur to me until now that he may have owned the joint. When I think back our valet seemed strangely vacant and blissful.

"The world is offering you things you don't need, it rarely –or *rather we* rarely– share our necessities." He was saying as we drank our coffee and looked out over the city. "But I'll tell you, its marvelous to get lost in yourself, to think your self a hero. The only difference is that people believe me now. They want to. They seem to be just as willing as I am to be lost in me. It adds a veracity to their daydreams, and nightmares, I presume."

Some time after my meeting with Kough, I had managed to stay with the girl. I was becoming fond of her, and she of me, as evidenced with the cabinetry, crown mouldings , and saw dust everywhere.

I had been hiding out in the house those days, content to sit around and write, paint. I had a job, nothing special, a few days a week chopping onions, washing dishes, listening to the ball games on the radio. Going home at night frozen in the winter and sweating all over canvases in the summer. I had been working on a self portrait for a week by then, unhappy with the results.

The country was in high gear, the nation had become more prosperous than ever before. Half the senators were for business, half for the workers, all of them preening to be reelected. But none could doubt opportunity was on the rise and so was the money.

It was around this time that I began to notice, the streets were quiet, people would plod along, not much anger, or malice but again, not much curiousity or civility either. Even at work the boss, who had come back from a professional forum, was now rather dull. There was no talk of money or production, we never butted heads. On the radio during games I would hear the announcer tell jokes, later in the broadcast I swore I'd hear the same joke again, delivered with new irony and finished with fresh astonishment. I thought the second joke funnier but the next week I heard the same joke, on the same radio station, three more times.

The silly and diligent workmen finally finished a new food market under the SlowLove trademark. The woman, my woman, and I went shopping, we'd joke and point down the aisles; all bleach would invariably be in blue containers, all the different chocolate in orange and red. Pulp fictions would be in shiny paperback editions always more than 200 pages never over 320. This was a Kough enterprise. And when the checkout girls, always smiling and surrounded by candy and magazines, went on break, I couldn't help but think that they sat there on halfwit couches, stuffing themselves on halfwit chocolates, reading halfwit inspired prose.

Jacob rang to say he would be back in town and that he'd like to talk with me. "Business", he said. I was told to meet him on a hill over looking the city. As I neared the summit I thought how apt a meeting place this was for a man who lorded over half the business in the city. It wasn't until a helicopter, like a small clockwork lamb chop, manned by a pigeon-eyed pilot descended out of the blue. And as I was prompted into the passenger chair -which was more like a bicycle seat- and quickly whisked toward the tallest building in the city, that I realized my mistake. Hill tops were for city lords. Kough needed a skyscraper to glimpse over his influence.

"Something to drink?" Jacob asked. The glare of the sun off the pool was blinding me. "Sure, something cool" I said. As my eyes adjusted, I saw them, pinheads everywhere. Redundantly netting the same area of the pool, absently cleaning, two ever so gingerly pouring me a drink. And in the corner of the roof, two boobs, biting their own tongues, were hunched over papers scribbling away. Over them, mouths agape, were two more blockheads with palm fronds crazily fanning away.

As I drank, Jacob told me of his plans. "You see it's very simple. there are people out there that buy, so there must be people that sell. I've made a fortune teaching my people, with care and diligence, to make things and provide service. Now to be more efficient I must teach people to buy. Do you see?" I nodded affirmation, but felt only warm sun on my chest, the drink cold, and Jacob proudly petting my hand. "All you have to do is tell them they are right, no need to argue, if you make it, they will buy it, but soon the very people who make it buy it and keep buying it..."

As I got home my stomach was upset, I went to the bathroom and pulled some antacids out of the medicine cabinet, chewed on them awhile, and decided to paint. As I set up the portrait I had been working on it dawned on me. Yes, I thought, the head was round, the nose and hair were competently handled, there was evidence of educated cropping, but the portrait was straight on. The eyes had highlights dead center of the pupils, the entire backround was the blue of a cloudless day. And the mouth, something wasn't right. It didn't wrap around the head properly, a small dribble of white near the corner of the mouth. This wasn't the élan of the brush. This painting was reported faithfully in front of a mirror. I had been drooling.

It was then the spell was broken. I realized that everything Kough had talked of was flat, placid. They did right, they were good but they weren't doing it for themselves. I realized one must do what one thinks right. Others' suggestions should be heard but not followed.

I write stories now for the homeless mostly, and some busy professionals. They help me publish some work which in turn they sell or trade on the black market. Some have approached me with offers of investment, a devout following of readers.

Others

There is so much I'd rather do

Than go to work.

I'd rather listen to music

Elegant, or rude.

We do live in a nation of excesses;

One can live pretty well off of the scraps of the

tenderloin

of entertainment

What is the point of working for others?

Placating juvenile egos?

Sure, I wish I had money.

But we got toilets

Books for a quarter

Roofs

Whiskey and wine

Bread and butter.

The Cat

The cat said to God, "I'm afraid that all the piety and all the faith won't pay off." He shook, "I'm alone and I'm afraid of waiting for anything."

And God said, " There are no guarantees."

The cat spoke again. "But there is goodness that goes rewarded if by, at least, my own recognition *yes?*"

The answer of the purple night growing behind black trees scared the hell out of him.

On Writing

Sitting here rereading my stuff. I think Hemingway had an advantageous notion, keep it brisk. Tight. Cut away the fat. Keep it light. I read some of my own stuff though, and I think, maybe I cut too much away, down to the quick, slicing down into the muscle. I've been reading Miller, of Anais Nin, the man gives me faith to go my own route. He's not bashful, going on huge triangulations , sometimes he rambles, the product of weak parents giving and giving, fear and nervousness. I grew up in a house where there was no warmth. Heat was made from ingenuity.... But I like Miller. I want to be able to just write, to read over, and continue to type away at the typewriter. Let the thoughts be transcribed into words then cooked down into something.

I like Buk' too, but I'm no bum, neither was he, I believe. It wasn't until the end that he showed everybody that he'd been hiding away his heart. With fear and anxiety you'd think he was born an old man, beating and ripping away from his father, but as death was coming and the glory came in ahead, the time to stop the fight loomed. He got in there and was willing to admit luck. He showed his cards—his hand was all hearts. He had more to give then, to me. The stories were just that, stories, pasted together with humor, drenched with fatigue and glistening with poetry.

Sometimes I wish I could just write. I could live life and just write. The closest I come now is going to work, looking at women, drinking, walking, riding the bike, sweating, tearing newspaper clippings, with the stench of summertime in Urbania, coming home and emptying my pockets of crumpled notes from through-out the day, sometimes written with such fervor as to be unintelligible, but the mind reads the scribbles and believes it to be something else, so that the notes of the event become an event in themselves, spawning something made of interest, confusion, humanity, although the word is indistinguishable, it is still tempered with the color of the event and the recollection of the day, the notes and the elec-tricity get away from you and your best is to just get some of it down. If you try to analyze it it just zooms away replaced by something else just as swift. And you're mired and slower by trying not only to react, but examine.

Sometimes I'm just happy being a mild native in light of all the things going around my head. It's tough to make a house out of broken branches, leaves from a thicket over there, connecting unlike things to get to some basics. The beer takes me away from the land of bullshit-on-a-stick, everything becomes linear and makes sense. I say, "Don't believe belief, believe the liars! They are the ones with the facts you need to stay clear of, or pay closer attention to. They have facts! That's why they lie. There is beauty and pain, love and hope… in the liar. The ones with truth are always happy. Everything appears to make sense to them."

Here I am in the middle of nowhere, in the middle of the night. Thinking. No-where to be. People outside. Maybe for an instant I see or feel a connection, begin to daydream about someone out there, it reaches a fever pitch then…

Then I slip back into the beer in front of me and I am happy. Right now. For no reason, against no reason, after no reason, reason slips back into pensiveness. Something made me think, whereas a second ago I couldn't see anything. I couldn't even wonder why I was blind to them. I feel like I'm moving in a forward progression, and then, for no more than a second, I feel like a fool. Like I've just missed it. The most important thing in the world that I shouldn't forget. I catch a glimpse of that feeling again and I want to kiss every woman that I've ever known and have them feel what I feel, or just felt then. I listen to music that I'd listened to before I had ever been with a woman. I was a boy until 21.

I became a man with a woman who had ended being a girl at 14. Before women I remember girls, the sea shore, florescence, my bike, wanting to give everything to a crush. Struggling through math class, and trying to look like others. To seem approachable. But my clothes always got stains and my face seemed always too real and naïve.

"JESUS" The cat is dying at my feet! I'm sitting here just typing and she's fading in front of me. Instead she spits up a katydid and meows at my face, pawing it. She looks at me, then at the bug under her paw.

After school in my bedroom, when my mother, somewhere between me and the world outside floating around downstairs, would be thinking. I'd think, about the window in my room that was only 15 feet up in the air, and that a door was down there with her. Anywhere was out that door. And she'd sit at her table with her flowered robe calling "Where are you headed?" and "When will you be back?" and the "Don't you have homework?" She'd just sigh and cross her brow. To clarify: she'd been judging. I was "wrong." The things I did were "wrong" She'd rather I stayed at school, fought to be like others. She wanted me to make sense. I was dazzled with the world back then. Anything was interesting. I was fairly quiet then, as I am fairly quiet now. I don't wish anything. She had her valuable lessons, though ones she wasn't conscious of, and she gave me something on the genetic level I could never pay back, even if I wanted to. Adults around me had the answers, they were sure. There was nothing else only "Don't be silly" Everything I ever said was preposterous. Well I'm 30 now. And I still look out windows, smell the sky and want out, and give away what I can't afford to.

Phlebotomy

Draining is
Not Painting
no writing
The day skipping its hours
compromising to the kitchen
To cook for the girl
She cuts herself, slips over into mania
sending you to the store
for bandages, Neosporin, peroxide.
To contending with other drivers' belligerence.

The only thing to ease the nerves
Is birthday champagne
A bad joke

Shopping to a dead greasy fool, crooning over the
aisles
Speechless about eternal devotion
How apt, I think,
But somehow,
I believe,
We see it differently

I pay the cashier
to the endless
clipped
staccato
Of Vangelis's
Chariots of fire

Horror

Mens' Life

All the modern technology only makes it easier to take and plunder,
so men continue to take and kill,
and piece something together,
make some thing.
small monuments.
as nature or technology
plot to take it away
and where they both fail,
then there are women
to whom men would give it all gladly
only to be plundered with less guile
and more efficiency then either.

Men's hearts are fragile and full of memory

The poor and the rich of us
all want to live forever
—or not think about it—
either physically
or through The Metaphor·
The Good Story,
The Small Concerto.
We're never taught to die—except maybe the musicians;
they make
and let die daily.
Constantly drinking beer, art, being alone,
are a survival instinct.
I wanna live, damn it!
it's a struggle to stay conscious
against
insanity and forgetfulness

Swillamette

Abraham was tired of work. Tired of living life between the cracks in his sched-ule. Fed up with chewing antacids and rubbing salve into his feet. Everyone at the job saw it as well. He'd start in with chopping top round and provolone in a dangerous over-hand fashion sending bits of meat and cheese flying.

The manager, Christopher, would come around making sure the entire kitchen could hear, especially waitresses and the other restaurant managers. The other managers would walk up and surround him. "Abe, champ" they'd say," What's wrong with you?"

"Nothing" he'd say, for really, the greatest feeling he had was inconve-nience.

"Hey man listen you're going to bring mice in here" then would come the cor-porate solution."Why don't you punch out--take a 30 minute break--relax, have thirty minutes to yourself."

* * * * *

It always sounded like a good idea but the reality of it was I'd clock out, as managers formed a circle around me, disappointed and shaking their heads. Deep down I didn't care anymore. I'd moved to Portland, Oregon, the middle of nowhere in the middle of this northeastern town full of hippiebumperstickerpoli-tics and pine trees. The whole town led down to the Willamette river. At night the rats took over, looting trash bins, fountains, parade leftovers. Rats had also been known to slip through the quietly delinquent back door.

I dreaded it all. But I did like the fact that they gave me a uniform everyday, no cleaning costs, but it was ill fit, I could feel the fabric stretch across the back. And the pants so tight they'd keep me from kneeling. I was sitting in the break room when Chris, the manager, walked up.

"Say man."

"Yeah."

"Why do you chew so many Rolaids?"

"My guts are twisted up from the night—too much" I made the gesture for drink.

"Yeah, I was going to mention that" he stared at the ground, then stammered. "Myself and the other managers are thinking, maybe you oughtta' cut down on some of the alcohol man," he smirked, "If you didn't work so hard we'd swear you drank a case before work" then laughed.

I said nothing. Got up, farted, flexed the seams of my coat, and went back to work.

* * * * *

The tough part was staying tough, I could still hear the decade long relationship, the perfect future. And there I was, surrounded by girls, young tight absent things, not conscious enough to take advantage of what was between their legs. Not wise enough to know that it will sag like everything else. So I continued to pop my Rolaids and stay clear of anyone who wanted what was best for the company.

* * * * *

Employee report 2291-49 Kough,A

I've broken my arm so I'm writing all of this month's reports on the computer—
He's a strange guy. I can't tell if he he's an idiot or too bright to say the wrong
thing. He's built wide but not fat really, but with broad shoulders. At the end of the
night he's seen carrying two iron baskets full of corn and apples. He reminds me of
a little horse. He's from Baltimore. New Jersey originally, I think. That's what the
manager said on his forms. His hair sticks out all over the back. And he loves that
bike of his. Big arms looked like he'd burst out of his jacket, and fast! He always
looks as if he couldn't care less but damn can he move food. I hated to admit it but
he gets it up and out, sells food like a pro, but always seemed preoccupied. I admit,
at first I thought, that he thought, that he was the greatest
—Arrogant—wanted to show us a thing or two, but every time we praised him he got even
quieter. Working and breathing like a furnace...

I couldn't understand how those guys did it. I'd try coming in, enjoying myself,
treating the place for what it was. Rent. The managers would come over collec-
tively scold us like children, but look at me with resignation on their faces? The
thing was, if I keep my head to the stone, stayed quiet, I was *disgruntled*. Did I
have to grin, teeth and back straight, in complete misery to look like I was working up to par? Slicing and charring myself wasn't good enough. What manage-
ment wanted was clear morality in its head, marked on its brow. "Smile buddy, I
can't bear to see you like this." That place was killing me slowly. So slowly no
one could see, or care.

Somehow I always ended up hanging around the dishwashers. Young kids
and Mexicans. To me they always seemed the sanest people in the restaurant
business. It's tough to bullshit the guy at the bottom. I'd try to watch their backs.
When I could I'd screw up orders and send the mistakes back to the guys in the
wet dish pit.

Ana was a soldier of fortune, willing to trade the hardship of war into the
horrors of the restaurant business, she had been a field medic in the middle of
south east Asia, a youth drunk with, then, French occupied South Vietnam. She
had met Mike LaMenton after the Americans decided to take their chances in
the rice paddies the French suddenly found themselves ready to desert.

Ana was a lush. Drinking and striding through the dining room while Mike
basically handled her. An effeminate man, nervous and picky, he had put on
the pounds since his days in the rice paddies and pea soup bivouacs. He now
had the habit of pouting toward the lights and tucking his great pink chin into
his blue silk collar. Mike was walking policy. A pure index of regulations and
procedure. A myopic shit with a tonsure of grey hair. I had not figured out why,
but all the dishwashers called him *Capitan Papada Pedrone*

* * * * *

All I remember from the accident was a girl, frantically combing her coat, and looking over her shoulder. She smoked a lot. Then I heard it over and over again, "objects appear smaller than they are." I couldn't remember if I saw her lips move or was it in my head?

I awoke to the sound of chirping. Mice everywhere. "oh fuck!"

"Who the hell are you?," a big one said.
totally incensed "Who the crap are you? I was hit by that car, I'm obviously drunk, see? and three inches tall, and talking to a fucking mouse!"

My head was killing me, a soft pressure in my skull every heartbeat pushing blood into the brain, two eyes peered through the dark at my two eyes swelling and pressing inside my head. I was prostrate in the shadow of a dumpster, a mouse came out of the black. "Hello there."
"What the hell is this?" I thought out loud, "A talking mouse. I must be dreaming. Please wake up dammit. I must be comatose on some curb somewhere. I can get someone to take me back to my bed, but damn it wake up!"
"You okay, boss?"
"Oh shit! I'm still out and the mouse is still talking to me."
" I'll get some help."
"You go do that, I'll stay here and wake up."
The mouse ran away and I laid my head down, closed my eyes and tried to wake up.
* * * * *
"Jesus, look at him."
"Get him up, we're headed back to the hole."
I opened my eyes. Now there were five mice slowly circling me and helping me to my–ah– feet. "This is crazy, what the hell is happening? Where's my bike?"
"Say buddy I didn't see any bike. You okay?"
"damn it I'm a man. you're a mouse! You don't talk. I talk."
"Sure you're a *man*, pal, listen how about a drink?"
"Listen, I'm a man," we all stopped and looked at each
other with incredulous eyes. They turned to each other and laughed.
"Well hell it's a dream" I screamed " and man or mouse I need a drink. bring me to your taps."
"That's the spirit, boss." A scruffy mouse and a skinny mouse each got underneath a shoulder and carried me into the night.

* * * * *

"So you worked in a kitchen huh?"
"Yes, it's a murder I tell you, every night at the mercy of another man's insecurities."

"Jesus, Abe, you got one hell of an imagination. You talk with such feeling , if I didn't know better I'd think you were drinking when we picked you up."

We were inside a bush not far from the water a bit underground. On the west side of the Willamette river between Salmon street and the Hawthorn bridge. There were pieces of food here and there, some spools of thread, a few bottle tops. Mice lounging all over the place.

" So you up for some food, boss?"

"Sure sure."

Off in the distance the bushes started rattling.

"Say, Abe, go see what it is."

The past few hours were fairly peaceful, sitting around gabbing, holding everyone in rapt silence. I stood up went toward the sound. I pulled back a few branches and stepped out into the park. I turned right then left and there stood on hind legs three large rats, eyes glowing, maws dripping, claws like shivs poised high above to attack. I froze. Struck with fear as I was, they growled stepping closer.

"Well."

A mouse shrieked.

"Well? Aren't you going to invite us in?"

Nothing registered. The only thing I could think about were the veins pounding in my head when behind me in the bushes I heard the high whistle of mouse laughter. From behind the rats the scruffy and skinny mice jumped out joining the laughter behind me. I realized the gaping furiousness above me was breaking into mirth at my fright. Then it hit me I could laugh too. The rats scooped me up and we all headed into the bushes, everyone laughing, including me at my own expense.

So everyone is drinking and I'm sloshed propped up against the fence chewing on old bread and loving it. There's a bottle cap full of grease and left over katsup. I'm eating an uncooked pasta noodle, a nice crunch, with a garbage bin aioli. And up comes to me a warm creature. I begin to desire. I look to see if we're alone. But it feels as if she's already done that. She walks right up to me and puts her paw on my face then runs it down my chest.

"So, are you enjoying yourself man-mouse?"

She didn't wait for an answer before sprawling out before me placing her head on my legs.

"Yes, this, all this is so... relaxing" I dipped some stale bread feeding her. We looked like some brisk drawing from Greek myth.

"Do you make up stories a lot? You're quite good you know."

"Thanks but this is no story."

She raised her head up "come on now, you're not that good." She sank back down her fur rubbing against my crotch. "You're right, I'm not that good."

The night was clear and a faint breeze blew the moon. Huge stars lit the edges of buildings and streets. No regrets. Nothing to do. Just my eyes, the female, and the light's lungs.

"Lets, go somewhere" she stirred.

I stared at the bridge signals and breathed.

"Come on, let's get out of here." I broke away from the night and looked at her and sprang from quiet into lust. "Okay follow me."

We were nearing my house, at least I hoped it was my house what the hell if I did wake up insane. A schizophrenic rodent that had delusions of humanity?

"How much furthur, Abe, I'm scared."

"Were almost there, come on."

"Abe, I'm scared I don't like this place. We're not safe. I can sense it."

"Get out of here, we're fine, I live here."

"Damn it, Abe, stop it, you're not a man and you never were one. LET'S GO!"

"Hold on, let's..."

"Abe, oh shit, it's a cat!"

"Where?"

It pounced on me. I could feel a wet nose sniffing me, and claws slowly growing into me.

The claws parted for a moment, I raised my head to see *my* cat. She was huge and smelled rancid. She lowered her head and hissed, cat spit flying.

"Jesus, Cat, it's me!" I reached my paw out and began rubbing under her chin.

The claws receded and the hissing turned to soft purring. I crawled from beneath her paws. The purring stopped, I froze, and again was sniffed. I gave her a chuck behind the ear and the purring returned, she crouched down for some more. I patted her back down by her tail, slapped at her sides. She fell over in joy. Landing on top of me.

"ABE!"

"I'm... I'm okay " crawling out from beneath my cat. "we're fine, it's my cat"

"You own a cat?"

"Sure."

"What the hell for?"

"What do you mean? She loves me."

"But you're a mouse."

"I'm a man" I corrected,"or at least I used to be."

"Come on, lets have some fun."

So we climbed on board the cat, me holding her collar and the female holding me.

Somehow I knew at this point that it would work so I dug my heels in as if the cat was a quarter horse. The cat sprang up and took off. The female clutched me for life, her small claws just digging into my flesh, huddling close to my back. I was truly the greek hero, I was Belleraphone, Tristan, riding an enchanted cat, 5 pounds of whiskered power between my legs, a beautiful mouse in the heat of passion holding my back. We sprang toward the river with lust-tempered fear.

A galloping silhouette against a black firmament.

"Abe."

We were near the river.

"Abe."

I was really drunk now, chest full of spoiled food and drink and lust.

"Abe! Pull this thing over!"

I yanked on the blue collar. The cat fell on her side. The female jumped off. I was too high. I slid off the animal, sauntered in front of her and began rubbing the bit of fur that grows forward on her nose. Her purr was simply loud now. She rolled over and stuck her legs in the air somewhere between happiness and retardation.

"Abe, come here."

We were across the river from the others. I could just make out the springs and the dark corner of the opposite bank that was the den.

"Are you happy?"

"Yes, very. This is one of the better nights I think."

I stood and looked across the river. The female walked up and put her hand on my chest again I instantly felt my heart reach out to touch her through my chest.

"You really were a man weren't you?"

"Yes."

"And how do men like you deal with that?"

I looked down at her and she at my erection.

I ran my hands through her fur I was awed by her tail how it glided this way and tha, her dark eyes seemed to draw me in, I could feel her heartbeat and smell excitement.

She slid her paw down, gliding past my crotch. "How do man's women do it?"

"Grab a hold", I said. Her little paws circled my penis, her claws just needling the flesh. I grew instantly rigid.

"Oh my."

Nature took over and she began stroking, her black eyes staring into mine as her body curled up against me, pressed against mine.

I grabbed her hind legs, moving her on top of me, easing her sex towards my beady black eyes. She pumped away at my cock. I could smell her heat and stuck my nose into that excitement. She instantly stopped pumping and went rigid. Her little pocket seemed so tempting I was in a frenzy slowly moving my mouse nose against her, then parting her with my little mouse tongue.

She began to squeak and shake. She fell on her stomach. Panting, her tiny ribs contracting. She looked back at me, closed her eyes, arched her back again then falling again this time without explaining she put it in her mouth. Choking on it at first. Then nibbling the end of my cock her little teeth and claws sending me into rapture. I was about to let it all go when I rolled over she looked at me and only one mouse to another, raw lust. I grabbed the scruff behind her ears and entered her from behind holding her down, then to the stars in front of the den. In front of the angel or devil that had done this to me. She squealed and panted some more I was a conqueror. I grabbed her hind legs and rammed it in on the end bending, losing conciusness. I bucked, pulled out bursting alive. She rolled to her back and stretched out. And lust turned to love as I climbed back on top of her. Belly to belly, heart to heart. I was inside her, she looked at me and I kissed her.

"Is that what men do?"

"Sometimes when they're lucky."

I'm not sure if they called the police or not. I doubt anyone is worried about finding me. Bottom of a lake or a mouse fucker would, I'm sure, garner the same concern. There are no more bicycles or windows, but for that matter there are no more cars or taxes for me either. When it rains the Mexican boys in the back keep dry bread and the bottom of choice wine for me. I suppose it's poverty that truly understands why we must share, and those dishwashers can recognize it in others. I still write and paint with bits of trash, discarded eyeliner, mustard, although I attain the same indifference from my audience, I suppose some things never change. Occasionally other mice catch me, looking out over the people, they think I'm pretending to clean one of the windows I've told them about, then I explain to them that I'm only waving bye-bye.

Alone

I thrive on being alone
Walking outside
I'm no good to society
Sometimes I fool them all, even myself
Caught between humanity and survival

I am a conquering lion mounting youth
With mothers 10 feet away in the next room
Stuffing myself on round little girls
while mommy sleeps
Basking luxurious in a midnight fog of booze and flesh

Tips on Care and Maintenance of Modern Prose

You see the artists with their black crayons
broken shapes and organs
listen to the screams of their outrage
and despair
damning everything around them
they say, "they're at the bottom"
"It's all shit"
but the ones that are really at the bottom,
the truly hopeless and lost
scratch their bellies and laugh

"I can save this"
I think out loud
this is a poem
meant to be a short story
but wilted
shriveled up and yellow,
tacked to the wall.
I am going to try and revive it ;
prune, and feed it
bring it into the sun
and attempt to revive it
both the gardener and the salvageable roots should be
kept warm and moist
with pots of coffee
and simple beer

Untitled II

I have no culture

No hidden handshake

No secret nods

Winks or uniforms

Maybe that's why I feel so alienated

Even in the kitchen there is an unspoken

Code of ethics

I run with people

That live without codes

So Hot Even Buddha Would Have Moaned

I can't even write tonight.
It's too hot for devotion, or even enlightenment.
I just want to sit down
And,
I'm not sure.
Do I even want to get a beer? It's so fucking hot!
I'm thick, and wet, and solid. A raw slab of bacon
stuck under the sun.
I just want to get something,
anything,
out of me.
But the best I can do is go to the bathroom and take a leak.
It's too hot for:
Women, who'll need things, but never are around when you need them.

Beer, to drink and slip into restlessness.

The cat, who rubs a black march of hairs across my calf,

or

Friends, that sit around being as hot as I am, never seeming to believe me.

Shoes, that make private puddles for my feet.

Beds, that I find myself in more and more, reclining
and agitated, without use or happiness.

Coffee, that will keep me up, sweating like the men
who picked the beans (only they seem to have purpose)

*—I'll think about not making anything, just sitting
here alone with no excuses—*

*Shit, this bathroom's like a battery holding all the
day's heat; my ass gets so soaked I can't even balance or read*

It's too hot for :

Being sad about life, I got it good, I should be proud,

Shit!

It's too hot for pride either.

Or staying dry.

It's too hot for lights, there's not much to see here anyway.

Or to hypnotize one's self, and believe that you're
attaining something.

It's too hot to remember that I visited my buddy and
that all the girls there were on me like a rock star.
Getting me drunk. Women, who were rubbing my back,
telling me how they were leaving their men for me.
Then letting me bite their nipples.

It's too hot to remember how later that night I ended
up drunk and insane. Fighting friends, and cursing
women at the bar, who called me a frat boy. A
beautiful frat boy,
laughing at me.

Eating and Drinking for Women

I wake up. After riding home surfing on top of a friend's woman's car. A meade drunk pharaoh giving direction with a wave of the hand. But again, I wake up. He's in bed getting ass. I'm on the roof of a car. I move to the couch, thinking about other days, When I'd got laid. When I could push my cock up to a woman at the least. I fall asleep, I wake up again, this time from dreams about bicycles.

They both walk out of his room promising me 'North Carolina ass'. I have become a virginal sibling and a charity case. "oh Jakob", his woman sings, "Amy called—" I close the door to the bathroom. And stand against the close wall pissing.

The sound filling the small room. My stomach deflating. I flush and open the door.—"she's so excited to meet you, but you must behave. And she can't wait and"—I walk down the stairs and pour myself water in a tall orange cup. I remember the beautiful dyke with the tattoos who I wooed the night before, red, sea blue and copper green flowers and dragon flames down her arm. Amber hair and glasses. I remember being told not to get into the car. Crawling on the roof screaming deranged—the cat screams at her empty bowl, at me. I put on my clothes and walk to the store to pick up the cat food, two hours of wandering and talking to myself, drunk and searching for cat food.

I think about love and the woman from last night, about some time in her arms. I fall back asleep until nighttime, head to work dishwashing for money. Read 'Lord Jim', and histories about America, I eat my sandwich, wash some plates and silverware and head to the bar for my beer. I head back home, back to my bar. I meet my buddy's woman there, sit with her at the bar. I order two beers, She tells me her disgust about tattoos.

A towering tightly shaved brunette walks up to me shoots a look back and says she's with the guy behind her, a midget. She's drunk and stumbles to the restroom. The midget comes up five minutes later, tells me he's with the tall brunette and stumbles his way to the other restroom. Two scotches are placed in front of me and my friend's woman. We drink our beers, I hold my glass up to the Chinese dwarf, and his three story woman. Two tequilas are dropped in front of me and the woman. We trade I take the scotch she takes the tequila, asking for lemon and sugar. At 2 o'clock the lights come on and we shuffle out, the little man with his arm around his woman's waist, his fingers disappear, clutching that big bald ass. My friend's woman and I go home. She goes to his room and commits air conditioned prayers for her man's deliverance. I go to my room. Turn on the radio, and put it up against the window fan. I think to myself I'm pretty good at eating and drinking that's got to be worth something.

History Wheel

Well, Kough,
Now you've done it.
What have you got to say for yourself?
History remembers Nixon, Mata Hari
"Kit" Marlowe, Sardanapalus
and remembers them all as worthwhile people
Who would care about a man that tried to ride his bike
paint pictures and write poetry?

you'll slip into the void Kough, with that crazy woman
of yours who brandishes her child
agaist responsiblity and decourum

You're dying, Kough
and no one cares.
You were made and wound without remedy or council
down here with these people creating hells for each
other.
The night always makes more sense for you
under a bruised sky
with half the world asleep.
—Breathing room—
we're working with hopelessness and no sense of
reprieve here
what's the plan?

Keep typing.
the sound of the letters against the platen
a common time beat
how did the gravel sound when a stick cut into it?
or the sound of a wet brush on papyrus?
quills scratching against the parchment
how did all the hammering, scratching, needles and
whispers orchestrate themselves?
what cadence my spectrum takes when
raw metal slaps inked gauze onto white pages.

For J"T"C

The man has had bad luck
It 'aint life
Or death, or genes;
The man just got bad luck.
A hard life, not the hardest, but a life turned
It back from the rest of ours.

If he was an egg
He'd be an ostrich egg
With a 4 inch thick shell.

Life 'aint free
For me or nobody
But with Tip it seems
Life won't even take credit or check.

Life and luck
Stuck a shiv in him twice
Once trying to gouge out his heart
second when it left it for dead wasted on
Washington Boulevard.

Wide like tractor tires
And a neck like the crest of a bull
But with luck black and worse.

With a body built for toil
It's no wonder he's learned the benefit
Of knowing no one cares.
For him compassion is like having four feet:
It doesn't make you twice as good a dancer
Imagine
Him down on the farm somewhere
When the chickens and the trained horses and the world
sleep
There he is on that fence
Sky colossal
A full moon night
So you can see everything not working.
The moon a reflection of his compassion:

It only shines down when the world plays dead.

His tattoo reminds me of
a heavy handed
Rendition of his life
Sliced open –again–
But by his own wishes

And deep in there is the same night
He saw as a youth
An immense space inside him
Like the one he'd look up at during the harvest moon
When he had a young bull mind,
In the huge night sky
While everything else slept.

Playing Love $\longrightarrow$

This is after a good friend destroyed a girl after their relationship.
Granted she was no prize, but it was difficult to watch what misplaced desire can do.

Love, and I mean carnal ownership, blind desire, is part of man from far before Hammurabi. Part of man that has no "sense". You wake up one day, and the words they say mean something else, they've traded up. Unfair? Well it is fair. Your bet lost, no matter what your angle. Be careful of love, worse than drink, depending on your perspective.

Broke and broken your whole life? Drink! Lie in bed, read, lose your job. Don't start with love.

Everyone believes they deserve it , but think, (now) you know better. You got all your luggage on the first day, don't start with love, Better to rent it.

No one likes to be lied to of course. It's like walking past a bar that smells as if the bleach has given up, but what's to stop anyone? Laws? Laws say: stop for red lights, but reality says we can run them. Lonely? Then call a friend. Horny? Make do like the rest of us. You're not special, and trust me, no one really likes special people anyway. You want to share? So give a bum an umbrella. Scared? Call a cop. Want a child? Teach third grade. For God's sake? You scream in that cloying high pitch of yours. And I answer, some gods would ask your life as forfeit for your virginity. But did you listen?

Here's my advice don't chain your life to someone else's. First, it's boring. Second, you have to savor a love no matter how short. Evaluating each persons capacity for it, it's better than throwing everything at a favorite. Otherwise you're led to the same unrewarding shame. Think. you've lived the first 20, 30, -and some lucky people- 40 years apart, What do you need them around for all the time? People in your life are like bourbon, you need just a little at a time, too much at once and you're all wet.

Shot Into Modern Medicine

Man would I like to go crazy.
Pack me up,
send me to the looney bin
where a white clad boy wheels me around all day,
regardless of my two working legs,
where they'd gives me paints and music
—artists aren't crazy they just want to be by modern
medical standards—
and talk in hushed tones.
And painting!—
they'd set me to it all day
to ease the suffering, of course.
and the poems
obviously the ramblings of a dilapidated ego
but get this: a healthy activity in the minds of
doctors and nurses.
leave it to modern science
and medicine to appreiciate music and art.
leave the job behind for good.
I think I could excel
in a mental health field
what's to get accustomed to?
No one gives me respect or seriously regards my work
anyway.
I'd be surrounded by young women
and some men
all making a living
listening to my horseshit.

25th and Howard

While riding down the street
On my bike I passed a young black girl
I remember driving past a girl just like her a long time ago
Thin and beautiful walking the streets with an older
woman, the pimp maybe. crushed under herself,
lumbering behind new beauty
I remember drunkenness and coercing her into the car
and the older woman warning her
The young dark girl laughed her off
And climbed into the car
She and I drove to my apartment
Lit by one light bulb
She was young 151617
And I showed her Freud, Bacon, books on Degas
She looked at them all
And then looked at me
Moving closer. Her perfect flesh
Like glass, no friction between her and the bursting
colored dress she wore
"Can I see your thing?" she said and started undoing
my pants
sometimes the most submissive have the most control
she yanked down my pants and my root was full
warm and ticking in the air
she grasped it
"Can I get 20 dollars to suck your dick?"
"Sure"
and she went at it
as I pulled up her dress looking at the young skin,
tight, she would look at me.
 I like your picture books she said gasping for
breath. " do you want to fuck me?"
I stood her up against the wall and pushed the whole
thing in
Pulling her dress over her head and forcing her
against the wall
She bent at the waist easily grabbing her ankles
I slammed her tiny body
My hands reached around her hips almost touching each
other
My thumbs on either side of her spine
And my finger tips gathered at her navel

`the smell of hot sex was all over my stomach and
filling the room
she licked her hand and wiped spit on my balls
she licked her palm again and again greasing the
wheels of the artist
I couldn't resist I shot semen and consciousness all
over her back, and the wall
And the floor
I gave her the 20 dollars she wanted
I scooped her up and we fell asleep together
On the couch
The next morning I woke she was gone the 20 dollars
still on the couch
Some people know the difference between love and lust
As an artist I knew the difference was that one was
full of potential the other closer to a job.

Smoked Shit

What the hell am I supposed to write about?
Shit. I can't remember a thing,
Sangria and straight whiskey can lead to nothing but
early death
And forgetfulness.
And as I turn up the stereo (I suppose deafness as well)
I was going to write about the faith.
About sitting there at the typer and making benediction
Somewhere between a platen a prayer and dreams.
A story was to take place incorporating the social habits of man
The humanistic qualities of animals, idiocy, some
pinch of Mark Twain and his correspondence with Aesop.
It was going to have something to do with the birth of
the pony express, the modern mail carrier and friends
separated by blue drop boxes

My hope and desire was that an idea, a literary
thought
Could be played out-- thoughts poured out in absence
of complete consciousness.
And the hours between sleep and rent could be spent
working through the vivaciousness of character and
plot.
through entertainment and lucky human dilemmas
But spelling and handwriting are the first and
probably one of the last human dilemmas.
Misunderstanding of a sentence holding the entire
human race back.

Then that part of you speaks up. The rough human,
in addition to every other thing that keeps going,
that keeps making notes, marks, words, sentences,
ideas.
Staying alive.

Is this what it turns out to be?
One against the world? That's very cold.
But sometimes...

Man! is it hard to transcribe listening, feeling, into
grammar.
-Espeesilly when you can't type worth a shut -

Whip cream with thumbtack peaks.
The world can't hear the click of the typwriter
The one thing that keeps me sane, coordinated
All they hear is the voice in their own heads
And the sound of the words
But they can't hear the sound of the tympastic
orchestration...
My mother said never type on the platen without a sheet of
paper
I still remember that from the second story of my mother's
house.

the pain of surviving
the 'versus'.
There I am moving type again.
Fuck Hemingway and his gloating.
We're on to huge amounts of information
Turned with the click of a button
We're a long way from Guttenberg and his fancy
shit
Any idiot can sit here and type
And convey his innermost thoughts, and lurid
unconscious
We don't need a God to be legible
We can sit here in the dark all over the world
Drunk, high, fortunate or famous

The pauper lot
Anyone can introduce the idea of themself.
Clear and concise
Brains get smaller and teams get bigger.
Christ! That gum jawed, piston armed hero was on the
mark.
I ams what I ams, and that's all that I ams.

The Artist and the Playwright

The Artist and the Playwright watch the awards. The little person on the screen accepts the statuette. The Playwright watches, leaps from his couch pointing at the screen screaming, "There they are, all the big names turning their form, their profession, into a horse race!" He looks at the artist, " presidential appointments, art, current events turned into sport!"

He lights a smoke edifying from the side of his mouth, "Leave the races to the professionals, let the horses run." He confronts the television again, "No one cares about the damned insane horses."

The Artist changes the channel. The Artist and Playwright watch the news. They watch the same shootings, the same consumer warning about feeding your dog garden mulch. The Playwright thinks to himself, there he goes again president Bush, still protecting us from the rickets ridden Arab hordes, and giving us all our money back. The artist dreams to himself about steak and a small salad every night. Beer on a table and wine in a refrigerator. And having it all after a three-day work week.

The Artist turns off the television. Sometimes it would be days or weeks between drawing and paintings. Sleeping everyday 18 hours or more. The only thing he could muster energy for, the only thing that made sense, was sleeping. Especially when the money was tight. And then the art would come like a torrent. He hadn't figured out how to turn the damn thing off and on.

The Playwright wakes, lights a *Black and Mild*. Puts on his sunglasses and underwear. Takes the stairs to the kitchen and pours day old coffee into a mug. The Playwright takes a sip and goes for the sugar in the cupboard. Nails, bolts, and screws fall out with the sugar. Onto the linoleum floor, the sink, his coffee. He grabs a bottle of rum from the refrigerator and adds it to the coffee. Stirring to the sound of ball bearings. The phone rings, the artist picks it up, the phone chatters, "Chefsohn is that you? This is Ha-" the artist slams the phone down. The playwright puffs his lean cigar.

Sipping his coffee to the banter of crows outside the window. The phone rings again. The Artist scratches his balls, stares at the device. The Artist calls the job, waits, answers, "Hello? Um. Oooh. I'm (cough, cough) calling out today"

"Chefsohn," the other end hollers, "Is that you? I just called there and you hung up on me."

"You called here? No, you didn't just call here."

"No no no I just called a minute ago damn it, I know it."

"Oh, you must have dialed the wrong number boss, listen I'm calling out, I'm married to the toilet and I don't feel well. Is that okay?"

"Fine Chefsohn, take care of yourself and-"

"Okay" and the artist quickly hangs up.

The Artist and the Playwright watch the television. The playwright turns to the artist, "What do you think about the Lakers?" he asks.

"I don't watch baseball," says the Artist.

"It's Basketball!"

"Who cares."

"Who cares about you!"

"I don't care about you either!"

Just then a news update says the president will be airing in a segment after the game. The artist turns to the playwright.
"What do you think of Bush?"
"A super-patriot and a xenophobe he doesn't like people who don't think like he does, or that dissent against the government."
"A Xenowhat? Say what are you a communist." The artist makes a joke.
"Communist?" says the playwright, "What decade are you in? They did away with the Communists. The whole worlds in it for the money. Now we're the only two well adjusted people left."
"Christ- we're fucked!"
"Listen," says the Playwright leaning over, "I was in that army that, that crazy bastard is sending over there, and all I remember was a bunch of arrested pinheads with testosterone leaking into their boots and a rifle in their hands. Crazy paranoid fuckers and meth' junkies."
"Jesus," says the Artist, "we're drowning in our cynicism."
"We have to, because we're not animals. They don't hold each other down, they don't take things personally, and they don't hide behind decorum."
"Given the choice I'd rather be in bed with a 105 pound blonde and a bottle of cold red wine."
"Shit."
The Artist and the Playwright sit at the bar. There is a small television on the wall. The Artist and the Playwright, still wearing his dark glasses, stare at their drinks.
The Playwright says, "Hollywood wants heros. It wants glamour. Something new all the time, while pandering to the attention span of a flea, it's hero worship, of Pop stars, Peace-makers, and killers. Social acceptance through letting go of the ego and pinning hope to a pampered scapegoat."
The Artist says, "It seems people listen to vacation music not so much to listen to it, but to cover up the swill gorged streets and broken ceilings a sound track to where they'd rather be. Why do people without consciousness always want to be in the sun? What do they think will grow in the sand? What's gonna rise on an island? I need culture. The islands are where people with no imagination go to die.
The Playwright, "Ah it's just talk, to feel better about ourselves, someone has to

make me feel better, shit, you think Dr. Giggles or that guy on the roof is going to do it? God does for those who do for themselves, but why blame him? There's enough here I'm going to shit or puke my guts out. But it's real, and wasn't here before, second rate or not, it's at a premium.

The Bartender walks up, "you guys okay here?" The Artist orders a beer and a bourbon, the Playwright asks for a rum, large, then calls after the bartender, "Rail" The poker machine and the television are pulsing auras and diluted light over the shoulders of patrons, there is a crash, as the Bartender drops the bottle of rum. The playwright leans over the bar lifts his dark glasses to witness. The Artist looks into the other bottles lined in front of the mirror and has visions of women.

The Fox and the Lioness

One day the fox went to work, and one of the lionesses was there, very beautiful, coat gleaming gold. "Hello," said the lioness. "Hello," said the fox, and promptly went to work.

"Listen here", said the lioness, "You need to go about your work cheerfully, and show me a little respect."

"Respect? do you really want respect?" suggested the fox, "Or do you just want me to get on my knees and crawl through your legs to get my paycheck?"

Moral one:
Groveling never cures the inevitable.

Moral two:
Going against one's nature feeds a belly worse than nothing.

Ten Years Fighting

Ten years fighting uphill.
I'm still struggling
Closer to living under route 83 than
A house in Remington, the west side
Or Govans.

You work all day and all night
No one will ever understand your
Unfortunate predicaments
Even if you live with them.

+ + + + + + +

A jockey died in Ohio
No health insurance
No life insurance
18 and going to night school.
And veterans are cowards,
Says the president
And his boys.

+ + + + + + +

My dreams of a cocaine
Actor handing me a million dollars
On drunken promises
Only to find me honorable
Even natured and a good investment
Died young tonight

I painted
Talked to the rich
Became honest and
A local legend
Well on the way to becoming
A much larger legend

Everyone was stunned
In disbelief
As to my upstanding nature

Talking
And acting
Thinking
Bullshitting
And feigning
Just like the upright

My best friends
don't believe it but,
I can be eloquent
Charming
Quite engaging
For money

Understand, I have disenchantment down
Might as well try acting "society"
and make a buck toward getting the hell out of this,
no?

I'm incorrigibly poisonous
Even the closest friends
Try me.
I'll live alone instead.
Survive.

We'll just Disagree.

Jack–O–My–Lantern

*A new Baltimore version. This is originally a folk tale written in
Maryland from a selection of stories collected by Annie Weston
Whitney & Caroline Canfield Bullock first published in a series
of memoirs of American Folklore in 1925.*

There was a man lived in Baltimore. Up near the Wyman Park, the man loved
to play guitar although he was not very good at it, not nearly so good as drinking
whiskey and National Bohemian. The guitar was a Fender six string, neck twisted
in all directions, tuning keys missing and the player was miserable, and that's
what made him content. All the people in town laughed "He's the happiest guy in
the world when nothing goes his way", they'd say, " never seen him so happy as
when his luck's fuck'd."

He'd drink then play in the dark. Sour notes, buzzing strings, he didn't care.
He had made them. And to him they always sounded as if they were becoming
something. It was vulgar and difficult to listen to.

And he hated authority, and judgment whatever. Living with the former: his
woman, wringing her hands over drunken misfortunes, ending up self appointed
governess of the spirits. and neighbor to the later. A whip-less fury and nympho-
maniacal finger-wagger, with a tyrannical religious reciprocity. A mouthful of an
explanation to be sure, a gilded mirror for that ever eating and enormous *corpus
monastica lex.*

But then again he wasn't of the variety who screamed at women. He'd slide into
them like a knife, "listen baby, I'm going out to drink."

"But I thought you were going to play guitar… here?"

"Listen, I'm not here to entertain you, I'm going out, pout all you want."

And he was off to the bar. Drinking cold beer and Jim Beam. Football was on
the television, Baltimore versus Philadelphia. The game was ending and the
Ravens were losing. He watched the rest of the game, and news reports about
stolen pensions, baseballers who shot up muscles, and Presidents who sent boys
to die. He drank more and thought about guitar, what he wanted it to sound like.
The guitar, to him, was mystical. Other people made it look as effortless as using
a shoehorn.he cherished it as if it was a religious charm.

Time and whiskey droned on. The money he'd brought slowly burned away. No
more booze.

He made to go home, he'd had his time alone with his thoughts. He was crossing
Charles street up by Johns Hopkins campus when the devil appeared to him and
said, "Jack, your time is near, Friend, let's go."

And in that moment Jack thought about the guitar, his woman and his drink.
"Listen" said Jack thumbing at the bar, "you came all this way… what d'ya'say?
you get one for the road, and I'll get one last one." The devil, a busy sort but not
perpetually tedious, replied, "Sure, sure—but let's make it quick."

Now just before they re-entered the bar Jack searched his pockets, "Listen boss,
he said to the devil, " I'm a little light, do us botha' favor do your devil thing and

flip into a fiver, we'll each do a shot then get to what's getting." Jack and the devil turned, Jack toward the bar and the devil into a solemn faced five dollar bill. Now when the bartender saw Jack again he was all smiles, "Jack buddy--more?"

"Two shotsa' Jagermeister."

"Two coming up"

The bartender put the glasses on the bar, Jack put the five up, and the bartender poured two shots, finishing the bottle. Now Jack thought...there's a cross between that stags head on that bottle, same as on its cap. Jack folded the five dollar bill slid it into the bottle and closed it quickly. "Listen, can I take this bottle?"

"Sure, I guess so , but who's the other shot for?"

Jack looked around. No devil. Jack looked in the green bottle and Abe Lincoln looked furious. Jack smiled toward his friend behind the bar.

"it's for you buddy, what do I owe ya."

And the bartender purred "come on baby, it's on me."

So Jack and his Bartender drank. Jack was completely bent now. So he headed home again, his new souvenir under his arm. Now when Jack got home he fumbled for his keys and he heard the devil in his bottle plead. "Please, Jack, please let me out of this bottle son, and I'll give you a whole year Jack, all to yourself boy, No bull, I'm straight just let me out."

"Well now I'm trussin' you Debil. I don't want to see you again till
Labor Day right?"

"Right"

Jack fumbled the cap and looked in the bottle but the devil was gone.

"Well", said Jack as he sat down on his front stoop," I guess I should straighten out. This night's giben me pause, I treat my girl rough, I got no assurances, I got no church, I'm a filthy drunk! Who cares about nothin' but hisself. Wastin' all day playin' my guitar. I'm done... no more." He quietly turned the key to the front door crept in, carefully put the guitar in the closet so as not to wake a soul, kissed his girl and with what seemed like a cold brick in his chest went to bed.

Now dawn broke, while Jack slept, slept like never before, only waking near noon. Jack sat up. "Man", he thought "I'm fucked." So he went to work, the boss yelled at him, the chef yelled at him, the whole damned kitchen where he worked yelled at him. "DAMN", thought Jack, I need a drink. So Jack drank. Whiskey over beer, and he drank like that after that vicious day at work-for six months. With six months left Jack became dejected again, "man, I've wasted six months worrin' about work, I'm a loser." So for six more months he played guitar, 24 hours a day, he played guitar. He lost his job. Angry and pathetic he continued playing guitar horribly and drinking late into the night.

Now the time had come to pass. Jack's year was up. And the Devil, anxious to resume his schedule, wanted to refasten his name in the annals of black arts and all things dark by finishing his business with one drunk, name of Jack, who hailed from the land of H.L. Mencken. Now the Devil strode through Jack's door sulfurous and cloaked in smoke. He scowled down at Jack "Fun 's fun" he said, "It's now time to make the leap, Jack." Jack, a resourful fellow- or at least a cronic procrastinator- asked the Devil for some small mercy, "Please Mr. Debil let me say goo' bye to my neighbor, just a few kinda words from her. I'm a d'unk, a filthy, d'unk but I'm stillamanwif-remorseses may be she could say a few kindwords and-

"I've turned men into beavers" the Devil cut in," to give them the impetus and ability to chew off their own nuts. Don't cross me boy!" so Jack and the Devil made a short pilgrimage to the woman next door. Jack knocked on the door and waited, shaking vigorously. "What's the matter with you?" asked the Devil. "This woman's been scoldin' me for years I can't imagine what she'll say to a animal like me." "Stiffen up man, show some backbone." The Devil thrust his thumb into the sky "For *THAT* guy's sake you're headed off with me!" Jack, with water in his eyes, looked up at the Devil, quaked pathetically, when a voice from within sweetly called for whomever was at the door. The Devil, opening the door, spoke, "Excuse us ma'am. Jack, your neighbor, was wondering if he could speak with you about—Well something's come up—the thing is." And with the Devil's head halfway in the door Jack sprang pushing the Devil through the doorway and shutting the door behind him. Jack etched a crude cross on the wooden door. the Devil howled, the trap had been sprung.

You see, Gloria, Jack's neighbor, was impatient with the lord and his ways and hot all over for the taste of male pleasures. Hoping for Jack but satisfied with her catch Gloria pitched herself headlong toward the Devil who found himself stuck behind a door he could not pass. Gloria, who previously turned to religion to exercise herself of fat and sexual demons, now found that she could exercise her fat with sex, and religion upon demons.

Jack, pleased with himself, went down to the Mid Towne Liquor, store bought a fifth of bourbon returned to Gloria's door, sat against the apartment and sipped golden bourbon to the music of the Devil's pleading.

When I think back to the event, images of gasoline and careless cigarettes, crocodiles, the Serengeti, my favorite cat and foolish mice come to mind. The Devil was remorseful, resourceful and ripe for bargaining.

"Jack, You bastard! Get me away from this bitch" he implored, "she's liable to ride me then eat me whole" Jack straigtened up and spoke through the door. "oka' Debel less' deal"

"Anything you want Jack, anything."

"I wants another year."

"Done", said the Devil.

"And I take my guitar whatever happens."

"Yes, yes you filthy shit, now release me!"

Jack slowly moved to the door put his hand on the knob. Jack flung the door open. The Devil vanished instantly. But Jack had no idea, he'd ran for his life. Now that Gloria had tasted of men, he was unconvinced it was safe to hang around.

Another year went by and Jack continued not to work much, he'd drink and fight, lose jobs, and somehow the guitar got worse. His horrible wailing, grieving noises eventually brought the authorities. Even the woman was done with him, leaving him in the care of whiskey and fleas. Jack was broken. With no woman Jack drank always, and didn't have the clean clothes to fool the public with anymore. Easy pickings for business with the Devil. And the Devil didn't fool around this time. Well placed drinks and a quick shot to the temple and the devil took Jack away.

Now the Devil brought Jack down to Hades. And walked him down the hall to his new abode in infinity. Jack sad at his predicament cast a forlorn glance at his new address. The Devil opened the door and Jack walked in, but the Devil was an entity of his word, there in the corner sat Jacks guitar. Jack entered and the Devil closed the door behind him. Jack pulled out his stash of bourbon put it down and hugged his guitar.

Now Jack had a neighbor down there in hell. Next door, an old man whose great sin on earth was quietly cursing his fellow man, little cotton balls of poison, sharp snowflakes from under his breath, whispered into his pillow, from behind closed and bolted doors. And the Devil had made him a great horn with the small end like a dog whistle with which to amplify his hatred and there by sing men to sleep with lullabies of intolerance and fear.

In the next room Jack was warmed to see his guitar again and, finishing his booze, with nothing to do for the next forever began to sing and play. Jack, as on earth, was thrilled in his pitiable circumstance. to be confined in hell, making horrible, horrible music forever.

Now the old man's horn was very sensitive and faced with Jacks tortured noises the horn emitted a very pervasive sound. The guitar was so bad though that whales began to beach themselves. Above ground, Gloria, the fat girl, Jack's neighbor near Wyman park, was dropping chocolate cake and squeezing Italian buttercream deep into her ear shafts while curled into a ball on the kitchen floor. The Emperor of Japan puked and considered supuku, at Pimlico the horses broke, with jockeys sailing, and bolted for the streets, babies cried and soiled themselves. On 28th and Charles. At the Med-Care South building, old men far past the scientific grasp of Viagra or hearing aids quietly smiled in senile silliness as a faint trembling, the reminiscence of youth and purpose, could be felt deep in their sun dried and long decaying groins. The trees dropped their leaves. Jack was playing from a song he'd wrote entitled oatmeal & shit or *every morning I wake up to the smell of last night on your breath*. This melee, channeled to Earth via the infernal horn, culminated merely from the first three notes.

Suddenly the door to Jacks room exploded open and there stood the Devil, hands over ears, fuming. The Devil prided himself on his candor and demeanor. Hell was a job, no reason to be personal, but a degree of discipline and regulation was none the less a necessity. The Devil walked up to Jack, lost in his guitars caterwaul, and slugged him. "Out you, out!" Jack stood up holding his head. The Devil cuffed him again. Little cobalt, green, and nauseous yellow imps gathered around Jack and began escorting him to the door of hell followed by the devils reproach." Do you hear me, this is a scandal Jack, you are a menace and an ass, Jack, go back from where you came boy, do you hear me?" " How will I find my way back in the dark?" Jack called. The Devil spit on a rock, which burst into flames, and grabbed a fresh skull from the ceiling of hell, placed the flaming rock into the skull, fashioning a hellish lantern, then handed it to a small minion with instructions, "Give this to him, and close the door. This is an outrage, that foul man is never to be found in my presence again." Jack turned his back on hell, "I didn't like it there anyway," muttering, "Who'd want to be where there's no whiskey anyway?"

The Animal

I leave the typewriter on all the time
just in case there is something to write.
It's as close to being alive as the voices on the radio
or the cat.
Sometimes it's hard to hear what it's saying
Sometimes the bottle
or bad fortune makes it seem more clear.
The drum of the keys against the platen
beat a march
The typewriter, my typwriter is a nocturnal
animal.
Active after the sun goes down and
the city has gone to bed.
Nothing may ever come of this writing,
but then again something tells me otherwise.
It sucks the things out of my head—
the jobs.
The heartbreak,
the bills, the wasted time.
It leaves me contented.
what's left is conviction and cunning

The Curmudgeon Escapes

I dreamt about love
real love
in a plane wrapped in blankets
and each others limbs
talking about coho salmon
and whispering love

I wake up
stomach twisted with poison
a dull rain
and a copy of de Sade
in my hand.

Union Memorial

Lying in bed
With nothing to do but
Take morphine
My "roommate" won the south Baltimore view
I got the little pictures of the pope
And a jesus painted to look like a lumberjack

I intermittently wake with different faces above me
Sometimes groups of them: doctors, nurses, students, a priest
All Dedicated, concerned, I'm sure,
Most born without humor,
Some...

But there is a sense of humor
they must have
That I'm trying to find,
As three of them spread me open
Shoving fingers
and aspirin up my ass.

Sweat and lube drench my bed,
Pissing scalding hot paring knives
And beginning to swallow again with
A bleach dry throat
I have t.v. , my copy of Daniel Mark Epstein,
the Sun newspaper, and more morphine

My hardboiled stomach
now has five navels
One from Ma
Then doctor cut two more for her cameras,
One for her knife
and one for my swollen appendix.

Now the little Korean nurse comes by
With the long loose curls,
Comes to check my wound
Pulling the blankets and robes far down
She looks down and we are both caught
She smiles and walks out.

I look forward to showers, shaves and restored dignity.
At home there is a girl seeking solace and crying over me,
But here at the hospital
lucid eyed poets... will
Sing no thrush song
Nor tune in Venus
Or reap lilacs for me.

Next

the bad nights

are when all the thoughts seemed forced.

And all the thinking and music turn out little

All the effort and all the past victories seem dead.

You wonder *what the hell is wrong?*

The lights dim, as if on cue.

And the job flexes its muscle.

Desperation and depression

Start straining your vision

A cold night when you can't even sense where things

will lead

Death and real victory near the straight grey.

Untitled III

Automated people
I can't fool them or myself
These sad men I have to work with
I trust my cat more.

At least I win either way
If I get fired I go home and do my work, I'm done there.
From our job in the open kitchen
All of us like a human clockworks

Pretty boys and girls
Breaking down calories while watching us.
Letting the show of human underachievement
Accompany their beef and chicken

The loneliness kicks in
Realizing I play second fiddle
To peoples lipstick and clothing,
And then one of the waitresses gives me a smile for
Broken chocolate cake crumbs
(All we have is each other)
It pushes the loneliness back
The failed engagements
I hope so hard, it begins to feels like glory

Depression rides me, so I pass the churning in my
guts into the pedals on my bike
And begin riding to work
Trying to get something to work inside me
Besides the veins

Then the job begins to be an inconvenience of other
people's convictions,
They think me aloof
But it's just apathy; there's really nothing
there for me
Being patted on the head like a dog at the kennel
Setting my watch by the quartz timing of the corporate "Thank
yous"
And the "Good jobs" they treat us like everything but men.

I hold onto my sanity with sarcasm

And my notes.
The cooked-up satire of this world's vocations
warmed over the idea that the streets can't throw me away
Jotting my notes, thieving every minute for myself,
Then stuffing them into my pockets my shoes my pants
All over my desk
Everywhere.

I suggest stealing but really it's sucking the marrow
Getting the essence, the feel
The brand of the word
At the same time keeping note of the spaces

Absently I run my arm along the salamander
The sound of flesh not fast enough to run
From the searing iron
I look across to the meat charring on the grill
(I think twice about steak)
Christ! I think, I'm standing here in line
Waiting to jump into the abyss.

And then I'm let off the job.

I begin typing frighteningly bad prose
Half drunk certainly,
and using the typewriter more like a piano,
making assertions about
language, beautiful women,
and the dead.

Weeds and marigold
Fresh hewn wood air
Letters and words
Arabesque all over the paper
Spinning smaller slamming up like meteors
Crossing slurring Brooooom
–b–to–e–to–s–
Sitting in the shade
Watching mayflies
And pollen
Drunkenly fall then ascend
Spinning

Fir trees climbing
Leaves in genuflection to the sun

Even the power lines and transformers glisten
Working for no reason
As the coniferous trees
Roofs chimneys and birds
Soak in and relax
And forget together
Under the dry soft sky

Below a black and white cat
Dreams, in color, of safari
Asleep in the shade of a leaning
Fence

Another Poem

Drunk and floating,
Tomorrow reminds you of an island
at summer camp
that always seems to stay
the same distance away
no matter how far out you swim
the water is deep
with things swimming beneath,
but the waves are so peaceful.
You flip onto your back
the water flows into your ears
and the clouds
drift by overhead
and you are drawn

Untitled

Sitting around sleeping,
the cat next to me,
almost happy.
bills at bay,
food in my stomach,
beer in the fridge,
chilled and ready.
I've even figured a way not to
go to a job anymore.
So luck does exist.
the news is either turned off somewhere,
or else neatly folded in the waste basket.
All I need is a woman
to work on,
and fall asleep beside me.

Song of the Wild Whistling Asshole

A rouge comes to the cheeks
Curling my fingers around the bowl

A
Porcelain
White
Knuckle
Rider

Either held hostage by a job—in a bar without a
crapper
Or unable to challenge the ladies room
for mortification of drowning in the odor of many
armpits
Or feminine ire

16 hours the intestines
Have moseyed a cowboy circle.
Sitting.

We all live like dignified Heroes
In the modern age of communication

The food now doing a loop-de-loop
In my guts:
Ham
And onions
Mayonnaise
Rye bread and rolls
Left over salmon
Half-wax ice cream
Butter, extra salt
Four beers,
And, of course, the coffee.

Sometimes I like the wait.
Clenched and sweating
Like that.
Anxious

To the point of nausea.
Waiting all day and half the night,
Like a kid,
Waiting for the explosion.
Bomb bay doors open followed by a whistle
Accented by hot and sour shamisen
Doubled with frailing banjo

www.ingramcontent.com/pod-product-compliance
Lightning Source LLC
Chambersburg PA
CBHW020330130626
46549CB00003B/1109